MACMILLAN READERS

UPPER LEVEL

NGŨGĨ WA THIONG'O

Weep Not, Child

Retold by Margaret Tarner
and approved by the author
Ngũgĩ wa Thiong'o

D1082523

Founding Editor: John Milne

The Macmillan Readers provide a choice of enjoyable reading materials for learners of English. The series is published at six levels – Starter, Beginner, Elementary, Pre-Intermediate, Intermediate and Upper.

Level control
Information, structure and vocabulary are controlled to suit the students' ability at each level.

The number of words at each level:

Starter	about 300 basic words
Beginner	about 600 basic words
Elementary	about 1100 basic words
Pre-Intermediate	about 1400 basic words
Intermediate	about 1600 basic words
Upper	about 2200 basic words

Vocabulary
Some difficult words and phrases in this book are important for understanding the story. Some of these words are explained in the story and some are shown in the pictures. From Pre-Intermediate level upwards, words are marked with a number like this: …[3]. These words are explained in the Glossary at the end of the book.

Contents

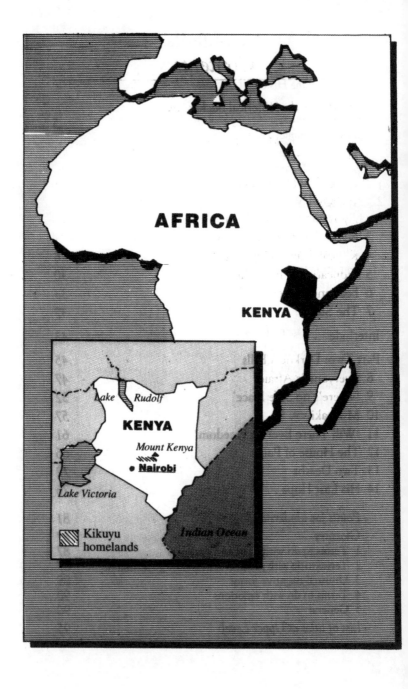

A Note on the Historical Background to This Story

This story is set in Kenya in the late 1950s and the early 1960s. At that time, Kenya was a British colony.

The colonial settlers took away Kenyan people's land. They forced Africans to work on the stolen land. They made many laws that were against African people.

The K.A.U. – the Kenyan African Union – was formed by black Kenyan leaders in 1944. But the British colonial rulers refused to recognize the leaders of the K.A.U. and did not allow them to have positions of responsibility.

The K.A.U. wanted to change the colonial government and the laws by peaceful means. They wanted to have the colour bar removed so that the black people would have equal rights with the whites; they wanted the land returned to the black farmers and they wanted black people to govern their own country.

Jomo Kenyatta became President of the K.A.U. in 1947. Kenyans believed he could save Kenya from the evils of colonialism. But the colonial government refused to listen to the K.A.U. The K.A.U. was banned and many of its members were imprisoned.

The K.A.U. had members from all over Kenya, but the highest number of members were from those parts of Kenya where the Kikuyu lived. Jomo Kenyatta was himself a Kikuyu. In 1951 a separate organization was formed from members of the K.A.U. Many of the members of this organization were men who had fought for the British in the Second World War. They believed that violence was the only way to bring about changes and to remove the colonial rule. In 1952 this separate organization, called 'Kenya Land and Freedom Army', or 'Mau Mau', began to attack colonial settlers. Mau Mau also attacked and killed Kenyan

5

chiefs. These were chiefs who supported the colonial government. Waruhiu – a well-known colonial chief – was killed in 1952.

In 1952 some leaders of the K.A.U. were killed and on 20th October of that year the government declared a state of emergency. Jomo Kenyatta was arrested and imprisoned, even though it was never proved that he was a member of the Mau Mau.

Many young people left their villages and joined the Mau Mau. Mau Mau was a secret nationalist organization and people from all over Kenya joined it. Most of the members were from the Kikuyu. A man joined the Mau Mau by taking a secret oath. He swore to fight for land and freedom. Members of the Mau Mau knew that if a man broke his oath or told anyone what he had sworn he would be killed by the Mau Mau.

The leader of the Mau Mau from 1953 to 1956 was Dedan Kimathi. Dedan Kimathi was caught and hanged by the British in 1956. By the end of that year approximately 2000 European and Asian civilians, soldiers and African government troops were dead, and over 11 000 Mau Mau had been killed. However, very many thousands of Kikuyu, including women and children, died of starvation and disease in the fortified villages. These were villages surrounded by troops sent in by the colonial government.

The British government was forced to give independence to Kenya in 1963. Jomo Kenyatta became the first President of the Republic of Kenya in 1964.

A Note on the Main Characters in This Story

Ngotho

Ngotho is the head of the family in this story. Ngotho works as a labourer on the land which his father once owned, but which the British gave to a white settler. Ngotho fought with the British Army in the First World War which is referred to in the story as the First Big War. Ngotho has two wives, Njeri and Nyokabi. He has three sons by Njeri and two sons by Nyokabi.

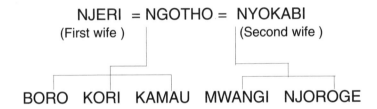

NJERI = NGOTHO = NYOKABI
(First wife) | | (Second wife)

BORO   KORI   KAMAU   MWANGI   NJOROGE

Boro

Ngotho's eldest son by his first wife. Boro fought for the British in the Second World War. He came back from the war a bitter and angry man. He has left home and has gone to Nairobi to look for work. Boro does not respect his father because Ngotho works as a labourer on the land which his father once owned.

7

Kori
Boro's brother. He also has left home and gone to find work in Nairobi.

Kamau
Njeri's youngest son. He has stayed at home and is learning to become a carpenter. His wages help to support the family.

Mwangi
Ngotho's son by his second wife, Nyokabi. Mwangi was killed while fighting for the British in the Second World War.

Njoroge
the main character in the story. He is Ngotho's youngest son by his wife, Nyokabi.

Other main characters

Jacobo
Jacobo has done well out of colonial rule. He is wealthy and is ready to help the British so that he can keep his land and his wealth. Mr Howlands uses Jacobo in his fight against the black people.

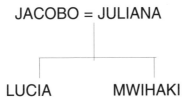

JACOBO = JULIANA

LUCIA   MWIHAKI

Mwihaki
Jacobo's daughter. She makes friends with Njoroge and falls in love with him. The unhappy love affair between Mwihaki and Njoroge is a central part of the story.

Mr Howlands
the white settler who farms the land which once belonged to Ngotho's father. He loves his farm and is determined that no one shall take it from him. His hatred for the black people increases as the struggle for freedom becomes fiercer.

PART ONE
THE WANING LIGHT

1

'Where Did Our Land Go?'

'Njoroge, Njoroge!' the woman called. The little boy, dressed in nothing but a piece of calico[3], ran up to his mother.

The woman smiled. Her small eyes were full of life and the smile lit up her dark face. She looked at the child with pride.

'Would you like to go to school?' she said.

Njoroge gasped, but said nothing.

'We are poor, you know that,' his mother went on.

'Yes, Mother.' The boy's voice shook a little.

'You won't get food at midday like the other children.'

'I understand.'

'And you must never bring shame[5] on us by refusing to go to school.'

The thought of going to school was like a bright light in Njoroge's mind[1].

'I want to go to school,' he said quietly. 'I will never refuse to go to school.'

'All right. You'll begin on Monday. When your father gets his pay, we'll go to the shops. I'll buy you a shirt and a pair of shorts.

'I thank you, Mother, very much.'

Njoroge wanted to say more, but he could not. His mother looked at his eyes and understood. She was happy because her son was happy. In the evening, Njoroge told his brother Kamau the news.

'Kamau, I shall go to school. I'm glad. Oh, so glad. But I wish you were coming too.'

'Don't worry about me,' Kamau said to the little boy. 'I'm being trained as a carpenter. It's a useful trade[5]. You get your education and I'll get a trade. Then one day, we'll have a better home for the whole family.'

'Yes,' Njoroge replied. 'That's what I want. I think people get rich because they are educated.'

Ngotho, Njoroge's father, was proud that his youngest son was going to school. Njoroge was the second son of Ngotho's second wife. Njoroge was the first of Ngotho's sons to go to school. A man was always proud if one of his sons went to school. It was important for the boy and his family.

Ngotho had two wives, Njeri and Nyokabi. They had given him five sons. Njeri was Njoroge's mother. She had had another son Mwangi but he was dead.

All the other brothers were friends and they often sat together in one hut. They loved to hear stories from Ngotho or the women. That night, all the young people sat together in Ngotho's big hut. Ngotho told them a story. It was the story of the first man and woman and of the land that God had given to them.

'God showed the man and woman the land and said: "This land I hand over to you, O Man and Woman. It's yours to keep and to look after for ever." '

There was a strange light in Ngotho's eyes as he spoke.

When he told this story, he forgot his wives and sons and all the young people in the hut.

Njoroge listened to the old story of the beginning of the world. He wished he had stood next to God and seen all the land. At the end of the story, he cried out, 'But where did our land go?'

Everyone looked at the little boy. Ngotho answered his son slowly.

'I am an old man now. But I have asked that question many times, waking and sleeping. I've said: What happened, O God, to the land that you gave us?

'I'll tell you what happened,' Ngotho went on. 'First the sun burnt all the land. There was no water and the cattle died. Then the white man came and took the land. But not all of it at first[3].

'Then came the First Big War. It was the white man's war,

but we had to fight for them. We had to clear the forest and make roads for them. We helped the British to win the war and we came back tired. We said to each other: "We have helped them. What will they give us in return for our help?"

'They gave us nothing in return for our help. Instead, they took our land.

'My father's land was taken from him. He died lonely, waiting for the white man to go. But the white man stayed. My father died on the land, working for another man. Now I too work for another man, on the land that used to belong to us.'

'You mean the land that Howlands farms[5]?'

The question came from Boro, Ngotho's eldest son.

'Yes, the same land,' Ngotho replied. 'My father showed it to me when I was young. But one day the land will return to us. I work here, waiting for that day.'

'And do you think that day will ever come?' another son, Kori, asked.

'I don't know. Perhaps not in my lifetime[3], but, oh God, I wish it was possible.'

Boro, sitting alone in a corner, thought about the land which they had lost.

Boro, too, had fought for the white man. He had fought in the Second Big War. That war had killed his brother, Mwangi, who had been his dearest friend. Boro had gone to the war a boy and returned a man. Now he was a man with no land and no job.

A bitter anger[4] filled Boro's heart. In a whisper that everyone could hear, he said, 'To hell with waiting.'

And to his father he said, 'How can you work for a man who has taken our land? How can you go on being his servant?'

And Boro walked out into the darkness without waiting for an answer.

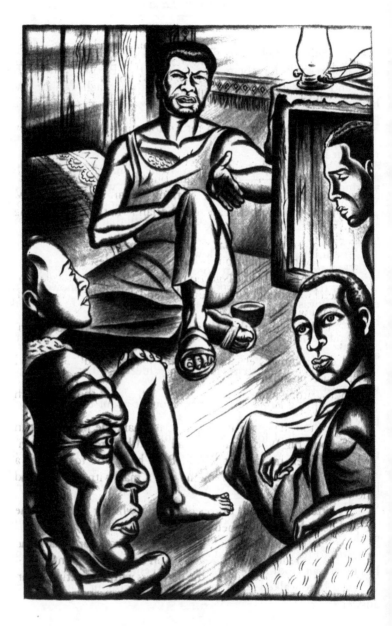

A bitter anger filled Boro's heart.

2

Njoroge Goes to School

On Monday, Njoroge went to school for the first time. He did not know exactly where the school was. So Mwihaki, the daughter of Jacobo, showed him the way.

Jacobo was the owner of the land on which Njoroge's family lived. Jacobo was a black man, but the white men allowed him to grow pyrethrum[5] as a cash crop[2] on his land. Pyrethrum was a cash crop which Jacobo was able to sell in the market. So Jacobo was rich and his big house looked like a white man's home.

Everything was new to Njoroge on that first day. The school was a strange place and the church beside it was the biggest building Njoroge had ever seen.

When the other boys saw Njoroge, they began to tease[5] him.

'You are a *Njuka*!' they cried. 'Come on, Njuka, carry this bag for me.'

'No, my name's Njoroge,' the little boy answered. He did not understand that Njuka meant 'new boy'.

The boys began to laugh. 'Njuka, Njuka!' they shouted.

But Mwihaki stopped them.

'Yes, he's a Njuka. But he's *my* Njuka. Don't any of you touch him!'

The boys were silent. Mwihaki's sister, Lucia, was a teacher at the school. They were afraid that if Mwihaki told her sister about them they might be beaten.

For the first few weeks, Njoroge always walked home with Mwihaki. They lived near each other and Njoroge liked the clever little girl.

One day, they did not go straight home. They sat down on a little hill and began to play. They forgot the time and, as darkness came, Nyokabi came looking for her son, Njoroge.

. . . as darkness came, Nyokabi came looking for Njoroge.

She was angry to find her son with Mwihaki. She did not want him to be friends with a rich man's daughter.

Njoroge was sorry to see his mother so angry. He decided that in the future he would keep away from Mwihaki.

Nyokabi was very proud of her son and she loved to see him reading or writing. She wanted Njoroge to get the white man's education. Then perhaps one day Ngotho, her husband, could stop working for Mr Howlands.

Njoroge told his mother everything that happened at school.

'The teacher asked me to tell a story today, Mother,' he said. 'A story you had told us came into my head. But when I stood up, I was afraid. I lost the story!'

'A man should not be afraid,' Nyokabi said. 'You have many stories. Or have we wasted our time telling them to you?'

'I tell you, Mother, I forgot all of them!' And the little boy's eyes opened wide.

Nyokabi laughed.

'All right. I'll tell them to you again. But now you must fetch your brother, Kamau. Your elder mother, Njeri, wants him. Don't forget to take off your school clothes first.'

Dressed in his old piece of calico, Njoroge took the path to the house of Nganga, the carpenter. The path went near Jacobo's house and Njoroge saw Mwihaki coming towards him. He was ashamed of meeting her dressed in his piece of calico, so he turned away and went along another path.

Nganga was the village carpenter and Ngotho had paid him a lot of money to teach Kamau his trade. Nganga was rich because he had land. Land was much more important than money. A man was rich only if he had land.

As Njoroge got near to Nganga's house, he saw his brother coming towards him.

'Work's over for today,' Kamau said. 'Let's go home, brother. Oh, how I hate this man, Nganga!'

'Why, brother? Isn't he a good man?'

'No, he isn't. He doesn't let me do anything. How can I learn a trade just by watching? He treats me like a servant.'

'But why?' Njoroge asked. 'He is a black man, like you.'

'Blackness is not all that makes a man,' Kamau replied bitterly. 'Rich men – black or white – never want others to get rich. Sometimes a European is better than an African. A white man is a white man. But a black man trying to be a white man is bad and harsh[5].'

Njoroge said nothing. These ideas were difficult for him to understand. But he knew that the only good thing was education.

3

Ngotho and Mr Howlands

Ngotho usually walked through the fields to work. Ngotho loved walking through the fields in the early morning when everything was green and the crops were in flower. But today he was walking along the busy tarmac road that went straight to the city. Black men had made the road for the white men in the First Big War.

Ngotho was thinking of what his son Boro had said. Ngotho thought too of all the lonely years of waiting – black men waiting for their land to be returned to them. Perhaps they had all waited too long. Perhaps it had been wrong to wait at all. Perhaps that was the coward's[5] way.

Mr Howlands, the white settler[2], was already up when Ngotho reached his land.

'Good morning, Ngotho.'

'Good morning, Bwana[5].'

'Had a good night?'

'Yes, Bwana.'

Mr Howlands always greeted Ngotho like this. But the white man's mind was far away. He was thinking of other things. He was thinking about his farm, his *shamba*. Nothing mattered to Mr Howlands except the shamba. It meant much more to him than his wife. She was a bad-tempered woman who was always quarrelling with the servants. She sent away boy[5] after boy, but Mr Howlands did not care. But she could not get rid of Ngotho. Mr Howlands refused to send him away.

Mr Howlands loved to see Ngotho working in the fields. He loved to watch the strong old man working. He loved to see the old man touching the earth and the plants as though they were his own.

Mr Howlands loved to see Ngotho working in the fields.

Mr Howlands felt that Ngotho was part of the farm. Ngotho could not be separated from it. When Ngotho had first begun working for him, Mr Howlands had had no money. But after Ngotho came, everything got better. For this reason, Mr Howlands wanted Ngotho to stay.

Mr Howlands looked like many of the other white settlers in Kenya. He was tall and heavily built, with a big stomach. His oval shaped face ended in a double chin.

Like Ngotho, Mr Howlands had fought in the First Big War. When peace came, Mr Howlands was no longer happy in England. He had settled in East Africa and the white government had given him land. A year or two later, Mr Howlands went back to England to find a wife.

Mrs Howlands came to Africa and she hated it. She had two children who were sent back to England to study. Peter, the boy, was killed in the Second Big War. The daughter became a missionary[5].

Mr Howlands loved his son, Peter. After Peter's death, Mr Howlands cared for nothing but his land. Later, he had another son, Stephen, but the land was all Mr Howlands thought about.

Like Mr Howlands, Ngotho loved the land. Ngotho really believed that one day the land would belong to black people again, to his sons perhaps.

'You like all this?' said Mr Howlands to Ngotho one day as they stood in the fields.

'It is the best land in all the country,' Ngotho replied.

Mr Howlands sighed.

'I don't know who will look after it when I am gone.'

Ngotho's heart filled with hope[4].

'Then you are going back to England – to your home?'

'No!' Mr Howlands shouted. 'No! My home is here.'

Ngotho could not understand. Would these white men never go away?

But now Mr Howlands was thinking about his dead son, Peter.

'The war took my son, Peter, away,' he said.

Ngotho had not known this. He wanted to tell Mr Howlands about his own son, Mwangi. He wanted to say, 'You white men took my son away too.' But he said nothing. He thought that Mr Howlands should not complain. After all, it had been the white man's war.

4

Kamau Talks to Njoroge

Njoroge was a clever little boy. He worked hard and did well at school. At the beginning of the next year, he was sent to the third class, Standard 1.

Ngotho was proud of his youngest son. And Njoroge himself thought that education was the most important thing in life. He wanted everyone to go to school.

One day, when they were hunting in the forest, Njoroge asked his brother Kamau, 'Why don't you start school, like me?'

But Kamau shook his head.

'No, Njoroge,' he said. 'A man without land must have a trade. One day I will be a good carpenter. Then I will be rich. I will be able to help you continue your education. Father agrees with me. He wants you to go on learning, to bring light to our home[1.] Education is the light of Kenya[1]. That's what Jomo says.'

Njoroge had heard of Jomo Kenyatta[2]. When Jomo had come back from across the sea, many people had gone to Nairobi to meet him. Njoroge thought that he would like to learn like Jomo. One day, he too would cross the sea to the land of the white man.

Ngotho told Njoroge, 'Education is everything.' But in his heart, Ngotho thought that owning land was more important. Education was only good because it would help black people to get back their land.

'We black men live under hard conditions,' Ngotho told his son. 'You must learn to escape these conditions. A man cannot live without a piece of land.'

Ngotho did not often complain. He believed that things would change in his lifetime. Ngotho believed in his heart that he was looking after the land that would one day belong to his family again. That was why he worked so hard for Mr Howlands.

Njoroge listened to his father. Njoroge knew that he was expected to do well at school. His education would help others. He would be able to help his father, his two mothers, his brothers and perhaps even the village.

'One day,' Njoroge told himself, 'something important will happen. And I shall make it happen.'

And the little boy's heart was filled with joy[4].

But Njoroge found some things difficult to understand. He often asked Kamau questions and his big brother tried to answer them.

One dark night, Njoroge and Kamau stood together on the little hill outside the village.

'Do you see those lights, far away?' Kamau said.

'Yes, that's Nairobi, isn't it?' Njoroge replied. Njoroge looked through the darkness to the distant lights. Nairobi, the big city, had taken away his two elder brothers, Boro and Kori. Njoroge could not understand why his brothers had left the family.

'Do you think Boro and Kori will forget home?' asked Njoroge.

'I'm sure they won't. No one can forget his home.'

'But why couldn't they work here? Why did they want to go away?'

'Think, Njoroge,' Kamau answered. 'There is no work for them here. The only happy people here are the ones with land. Boro has no land. He couldn't get work here. And Boro is angry with our father because he works for another man. Boro is angry with all the older men who let the white men take the land.'

'What does our father say?'

'He says that the black men did try to get the land back after the Second Big War. But they failed.'

'And does Boro blame[5] our father for this?'

'I think so. Boro's heart is full of hate[4] for the white men. He blames the British for the death of our brother, Mwangi. The war and the fighting changed Boro. He has become a strong and angry man. Perhaps he is stronger than our father. I sometimes think that our father is afraid of Boro.

The two brothers stood looking at the lights of the city, the city that had taken away their brothers.

'I would like to go to Nairobi too,' Kamau said softly.

'I'm a good enough carpenter now to get a job in the city.'

'What about the strike[5] that father has been talking about? If the black people in Nairobi go on strike, no one will work.'

'I don't know,' said Kamau. 'Father thinks the strike will help us, but I'm not sure.'

'Father says the strike is for all people who want freedom,' Njoroge said. 'Father says the black people are striking to get their land back. He says that all this land belongs to the black people. Do you think that is true, Kamau?'

'Yes of course. The land is ours. The white men from England stole it from us. They are all thieves; Mr Howlands is a thief.'

'I don't like Mr Howlands,' Njoroge said quietly. 'His son followed me once and I was afraid. He was a tall, thin boy, with yellow hair.'

Njoroge stood in silence for a minute and then he said, 'Kamau, tell me about Jomo. Who is he?'

'Boro called him the Black Moses.'

'I've heard about Moses,' Njoroge said. 'He is in the Bible. He led his people to the land God had given them.'

Later that night, before he went to sleep, Njoroge thought about the future. He did not want to work for a white man. Yes, he, Njoroge, would be different from his father. Before he went to sleep, he prayed.

'Oh, God, let me get the white man's learning. I want to help my father, my two mothers and all my brothers . . .'

And the little boy fell asleep and dreamt of education – in England.

'I would like to go to Nairobi too,' Kamau said softly.

5

'Education is Everything'

When he reached Standard 4, Njoroge began to learn English. He was now in the same class as Mwihaki. Their teacher was Lucia, Mwihaki's sister.

The two children tried hard to learn English. It was important for them to learn English. But it was difficult and sometimes Njoroge got confused.

'I am standing up,' the teacher said. 'What am I doing?'

'You are standing up,' the class replied. Lucia pointed her finger.

'You, boy, what's your name?'

'Njoroge.'

'Stand up, Njoroge. Now, what are you doing?'

Njoroge was afraid of the watching, smiling faces.

'You are standing up,' he said.

'No, no. What are *you* doing?'

Njoroge answered again, 'You are standing up.' The teacher was really angry now. She told Mwihaki to stand too.

'Mwihaki, what are you doing?'

'I am standing up.'

'Good. Now, Njoroge. What is she doing?'

'I am standing up.'

The pupils laughed quietly. But when the teacher asked them, they could not give the right answer.

'Look here, you lazy, stupid fools!' Lucia shouted. 'We did all this yesterday. If you make just one mistake tomorrow, I'll beat you all!' But in the end, the children understood.

After a while, when a teacher came into the class, they could speak to him in English.

'Good morning, children,' he said.

'Good morning, sir,' the children answered.

One day, a white woman came to the school. The school was made clean and tidy. All the children were told what to say and do.

Njoroge had not been so near to a white woman before. The whiteness and softness of her skin surprised him.

The class stood up, ready to greet her.

'Good morning, children.'

'Good morning, sir.'

Lucia felt like crying. The children had forgotten everything she had told them.

'I am a woman, so you must call me "Madam",' the white woman explained. 'And it is after lunch now, so you must say "afternoon". Do you understand?'

'Yes, sir,' they all cried.

'Madam! Madam! Say Madam!' Lucia shouted at them.

'Good afternoon, Madam.' But some of them still said, 'Sir'.

When the white woman had gone, Lucia beat all the children and they were sorry. In this way, they learnt the difference between 'Sir' and 'Madam', and between 'morning' and 'afternoon'.

Njoroge found out later that the white woman, who was a missionary, was Mr Howlands' daughter. This surprised Njoroge. The white settlers, like Mr Howlands, thought that they were better than the black men. But missionaries said that the black people were as good as white people.

Perhaps she's different from her father, Njoroge thought.

———

At about this time, Kamau stopped working for Nganga. He began to work as a carpenter in one of the African shops in the nearby village of Kippanga. Kamau didn't go to Nairobi and this made

Njoroge happy. But Njoroge was still afraid that one day Kamau would go and join his brothers, Kori and Boro, in Nairobi.

The two brothers came home often, but they were changing. Kamau did not change. He was still part of the family. If Kamau left, the family would be broken.

Njoroge often went to Kippanga to see his brother. The African shops in the village were miserable looking places. The work was hard and boring. The young men who worked in the shops looked sad and bored. The sight of these sad young men made Njoroge work harder in school. Education was the thing that would give him a different future. Education was the key to a better life.

Books were Njoroge's best friend. He read everything he could, but the Bible was his favourite book. The Bible, and the stories his mother told him, all seemed to say the same thing. If a man was good, God would reward[5] him. Bad things happened to bad men.

Njoroge remembered his brother saying that Jomo was the Black Moses. Njoroge thought he understood this now. If Jomo was like Moses, then black men were the chosen people of God[5].

Njoroge believed that the future of his family and his village depended on two things – his education and his belief in God.

Whenever he was with Mwihaki, Njoroge tried to tell her about these things. But he was not able to explain his ideas. He could not think of the right words. So Njoroge kept his thoughts to himself. The tall, brown-skinned, clear-eyed boy walked alone in the fields and kept his ideas in his own heart[5].

6

Fear and Anger

When the elders of the village[5] talked with Ngotho, they sometimes sat in the hut of either Nyokabi or Njeri. Then Njoroge was happy because he could sit there and listen to them.

When Kori and Boro came home on a visit, they sometimes brought home young men from the city. These young men seemed to know a lot of things. When they talked, they did not laugh and joke as young men usually did. They talked about war, unemployment[2] and stolen land. And when they talked, the elders listened.

They often talked about Jomo. Njoroge had read the Bible. In the Bible, he had read about Moses and how Moses had lead the Children of Israel to the Promised Land. Njoroge believed that when the young men talked about Jomo they were really talking about Moses. Njoroge believed that the black people were the Children of Israel and Jomo was going to lead them to the Promised Land.

The young men also talked about the coming strike. All the black men who worked for white men or the government were going to go on strike. The strikers would show the white men that the black men were not slaves. The black people had children to feed and educate, just like the white men.

'Everyone will go on strike,' someone said. 'Every black man everywhere, even policemen and soldiers. Black men are all brothers.'

'Shall we get the same pay as Indians and Europeans?'

'Yes. It is us, the black people, who do all the hard work. Business depends on us. We will demand more money. We cannot live on the money we get now.'

Everyone listened. They didn't know much about strikes, but they all wanted more money.

That night, Njoroge prayed that the strike would be a success. Then he fell asleep. He dreamt of the money and happiness that they would all have after the strike.

When Mr Howlands heard about the strike, he called all his workers together. He told his workers that anyone who went on strike would lose his job. He would not allow a strike to stop the work on his farm!

Ngotho listened to Mr Howlands. His face did not show his thoughts. Ngotho could not make up his mind[5] about the strike. It might fail.

If he lost his job, the land would never be his. After the meeting, Ngotho did not talk to the other men. He went straight home.

To Njoroge, his father Ngotho was the centre of everything. As long as Ngotho lived, nothing could go wrong. Njoroge feared his father, but he trusted him too. Ngotho was well-known as a man who could keep his family together.

But thinking about the strike had confused Ngotho. Fear of losing his land gripped him. And this fear slowly turned to anger.

When Njoroge came back from school that day, he found Nyokabi crying. Ngotho, tall and strong in spite of his age, stood in front of her. His face was full of anger.

'I must be a man in my own house!' Ngotho was shouting.

'Yes, be a man and lose your job! And then we shall all starve!'

'I shall do what I like. I have never taken orders from a woman,' Ngotho shouted. 'This strike is important for all black people. Why must I work for a white man and his children? We need more money and the strike will give it to us!'

But Nyokabi knew that Ngotho was shouting because he was afraid.

'What if the strike fails? Tell me that!' she cried.

'Shut up!' Ngotho shouted. He slapped Nyokabi's face and raised his hand again.

Njoroge, terribly afraid, ran forward.

'Please, Father!' he cried.

Ngotho grabbed Njoroge by the shoulders. Ngotho began to speak, but changed his mind[5]. He let the boy go and walked out of the hut.

Njoroge tried to comfort[5] his mother, but she went on crying.

'Why have they bewitched[5] him? My man is changed . . .'

That night, Njoroge felt more alone than ever. He did not know who was right – his father or his mother. He prayed for them both and then he asked God a question.

'Oh, God, do you think the strike will be a success?'

Njoroge waited in the dark for God's answer, and, while he was waiting, fell asleep.

'Shut up!' Ngotho shouted. He slapped Nyokabi's face.

7

The Strike

It was the beginning of New Year. Njoroge had been at school for five years. He sat in the big classroom with Mwihaki and all the other pupils. The class was waiting to hear whether they had passed their exams or not.

The teacher came in with the list of names. Njoroge wanted to hide under a desk. And then he heard his name. He was the first in the class. Mwihaki had passed too. They would both be going to a new school.

Together they ran home, hand in hand. Each wanted to tell their parents the good news. When they came near Mwihaki's house, they stood together for a moment. Then ran off along their different paths.

Mwihaki reached home first.

'Mother! Mother!' she cried.

But her mother looked at her coldly.

'What is it?' she said. 'What has happened now?'

'Nothing,' Mwihaki whispered, 'only that I have passed.'

'Is that all?' her mother said. Then she cried out, 'A man will never listen to a woman! I told him not to go.'

'What has happened, Mother?'

'What a question! I've always said your father will be murdered one day.'

'What, is he dead?' Mwihaki burst out crying, but no one answered her.

When Njoroge reached home, the open place near the huts was full of people. Some of them were looking towards his father's hut and others were turned towards the market-place. Njoroge found his mother, Nyokabi, in her hut. Two village women were sitting with her and she was crying quietly. Njoroge forgot his good news.

Had someone died?

'What is it, Mother?' he asked.

'It's the strike,' the women told him.

Yes, it was the first day of the strike – the strike that was going to stop the whole country! And Njoroge had forgotten. He ran to his brother Kamau, who told him what had happened.

A meeting had been held on the first day of the strike. Many people had gone to it and Ngotho had been one of them.

Speakers had come from Nairobi, including a young man whom Boro had brought to the village. Boro was sitting on the platform with the young man and Ngotho was proud to see him there.

The young man got up to speak. He reminded them of the time when the land had belonged to the black people. Africa was theirs because God had given it to them. Then the white man had come and taken the land away from them.

'How foolish our fathers were to believe them!' the young man cried. 'Our fathers were taken away to fight in the First Big War– the white man's war. And when our fathers came back their land had been given to the white men! Was that fair? (No! No!) The black people were forced to work for them and pay taxes[2]. Where did their freedom go?

'When the Second Big War came, then we were taken away to fight. Black men died to save the British Empire[2]. Was that fair? (No! No!) But we cried aloud to God and God heard us. He sent a man to us called Jomo. He was our Black Moses. He told the white men: "Let my people go!" '

The young man's voice was raised to a shout.

'And that's why we are here today. All black men are brothers. Together we must cry with one voice: "The time has come! Let my people go! We want our land – now." '

Ngotho listened, unhappy and confused. He could not shout, but he heard others shouting. For a few minutes, his eyes were full of tears and he could not see clearly. Then he realized that the whole meeting was surrounded by policemen. They were standing quietly, with heavy sticks in their hands.

The speaker went on. 'Remember, this must be a peaceful strike. We must get more pay. But there must be no violence. If you are hit, don't hit back!'

At that moment, a white police inspector got onto the platform. And with him – Jacobo! Why was Jacobo standing next to a white man? Then, when Jacobo began to speak, Ngotho understood.

Jacobo, the richest black man in all the land around, was speaking for the white people! He was telling everyone to go back to work. They listened in silence.

As Ngotho listened, something happened to him. Not all black men were brothers, for here was Jacobo – and he was a traitor[2].

Ngotho thought of all the long years of waiting and suffering. Slowly, he began to move towards the platform. Then he was standing right in front of Jacobo. The two black men faced each other. The battle was now between these two – Jacobo on the side of the white people and Ngotho on the side of the black people.

Ngotho turned and in a terrible voice cried: 'Arise!'

The crowd moved forward. Led on by Ngotho's cry, they rushed towards Jacobo. The police attacked with guns and tear-gas[5].

Ngotho ran about blindly in the crowd. His courage had gone and he was full of fear. A policeman hit him in the face, but he ran on. Feeling the blood flow, he ran faster, stumbled and then fell.

People from his village found him where he lay unconscious. They carried him home. Ngotho was the hero of the hour[5].

Days later, people were still talking about Jacobo and Ngotho.

'The old man is brave . . .'

'He is, to be sure. But why did he do it? He caused the death of two men.'

Ngotho turned and in a terrible voice cried: 'Arise!'

'Ah, but he had to do something. Who could listen to a black man saying these things?'

'Jacobo is a traitor. You know how he got so rich.'

'Yes! He sold us, his brothers, to the white man!'

'Yes, yes,' several voices agreed.

But one man shook his head sadly.

'Ngotho has only harmed himself,' he said. 'He has been told to leave Jacobo's land.'

'Leave Jacobo's land? But Ngotho was there before Jacobo bought it! It is against the custom[2].'

The men began to shout but then they saw a policeman coming towards them. They moved away quietly. It was clear now that the strike had failed.

Now Ngotho found out who his friends were. Nganga, the carpenter, gave him a place to build new huts. But new huts cost money and Ngotho had no job.

Things became difficult for Njoroge. Fees were higher in his new school. Mwihaki, Jacobo's daughter, was sent to a boarding school far away. She would go on learning, but Njoroge would have to stop.

Njoroge cried and he prayed to God. And God heard his prayers. Kamau's wages were raised and he gave the money to Njoroge. Kori gave the rest of the money. Njoroge was glad. He too would go on learning.

INTERLUDE

Two and a half years later, a disillusioned[5] government official stood on a hill, looking down at Nairobi. He was looking down at the country he would soon be leaving. He looked down at the city that the white man had made. The city was where all the trouble came from.

How did this trouble start? Could I have guessed there would be trouble? No, there were no signs to tell me. Or, were there signs and I didn't see them?

We tried our best. We tried to help them. Now we are leaving. Leaving without thanks.

————

The people passed on news. Sometimes they heard it on a neighbour's radio. Sometimes their friends told them.

Listen, neighbour, a great chief has died.

What's that to me? My children are crying for food.

But he was a big chief. It's an interesting story.

A big chief like Jacobo?

Bigger. And he was killed in daylight.

That was daring. Tell me. Tell us all.

. . . The Government had given this chief much land. In return, the chief had sold his own people. This chief was driving to Nairobi, when two men followed him. In a quiet place, they made the chief's car stop. They shot the chief three times. When he was dead, they drove away . . .

They were brave . . .

They learnt this trick from the white man . . .

They were brave, those young men . . .

————

Then one night, Jomo Kenyatta and all the leaders of the land were arrested.

But they can't arrest Jomo! Now we are without a leader.

Yes, that's what they want . . .

A state of emergency was declared.

A state of emergency? What's that?

Don't you know? It means we can do nothing. We are all prisoners in our own land.

———

Njoroge had never seen Jomo. Once, he had gone to a meeting where Jomo had been speaking. Jomo had spoken about freedom and about the trouble the colour-bar had made in Kenya.

Njoroge had heard all about the colour-bar from his brothers in Nairobi. He did not know what it was really. But he knew that the strike had failed because of the colour-bar. Black people had no land because of the colour-bar. And they could not eat in hotels because of the colour-bar. The colour-bar was everywhere.

Njoroge had gone early to the meeting-place in order to see Jomo. But there were so many people there that Njoroge was unable to see Jomo. And now Jomo had been arrested. Perhaps Njoroge would never see him now . . .

PART TWO
DARKNESS FALLS

8

Everyone is Afraid

And now stories began to spread about the land, passed on by many voices. Njoroge listened carefully to them all.

Many of these stories were about Dedan Kimathi, leader of the African Freedom Army[2]. In the stories, Kimathi was able to turn himself into any shape – a bird, an aeroplane or even a white policeman. The country was full of stories and rumours[5] and they brought the people together.

Many things had changed. Jacobo had been made a chief. He lived in fear of Mau Mau, the Freedom Boys of the Forest[2]. Two policemen with guns always walked with him. Sometimes he moved around with the new District Officer[2], who was Mr Howlands.

Njoroge's family now lived in three rough huts on Nganga's land. Ngotho had no job; only Kori and Kamau brought money home.

Njoroge had been at his new school for two years. Every day he walked five miles to school and five miles back. That is what education meant to him and to thousands of boys and girls all over Kenya.

It was dark when Njoroge reached home that day. Njoroge felt cold and hungry, but there was no smell of food being cooked.

He heard voices from Njeri's hut and went in. Ngotho was there with the family and Njoroge sat down without being told. As he looked around the dark hut, Njoroge saw his brother, Boro.

'How is it with you, brother? We have not seen you here for a long time.'

'It is well, brother. How is school?'

'It's all well. I hope you left Kori in peace.'

'Oh, dear child, we all hope so,' his father said.

'How can we hope?' Njeri cried out. 'He and many others have been taken!'

'Oh, if they should kill him!' Boro cried out.

At that moment, the door opened and Kori staggered into the hut. His face was thin and he could hardly stand.

'Water! Food!' he cried.

When he was strong enough, he told his story.

Kori began. 'Many, many young men have been imprisoned as terrorists,' Kori began. 'You were lucky to escape, Boro.'

'What about you? How did you . . .?'

'After you escaped,' Kori answered, 'the police beat us and put us into trucks. I think they planned to kill us. So when the truck slowed down, I jumped out and escaped into the forest. They fired at me, but they didn't hit me. I got a lift in a lorry and somehow managed to get home.'

'Why are these things happening to the black people?' Njeri asked.

'They want us weak before Jomo gets out of prison. They are afraid because they know he will win his case[2].'

'So if Jomo wins, will they let everyone out of prison?'

'Of course. And then we will have Freedom.'

Ngotho sat in the corner of the hut, saying nothing. Since the strike, he had changed. Boro had told his father that his attack on Jacobo had spoilt everything. Boro no longer respected his father. Ngotho had lost his importance in the family.

But there was one thing Ngotho would not do. He would not take the Mau Mau oath[2] from his son. Ngotho was not against taking oaths. Oaths drew people together. But how could any man take oath from his son? Such a thing was against all custom and tradition.

But Mau Mau was gaining supporters every day. They were

'When the truck slowed down, I jumped out and escaped.'

the Freedom Boys of the Forest. A boy at school had told Njoroge
about them.

'Mau Mau is a secret tribe which you join by "drinking oath".
Then you become a soldier with Kimathi as your leader.'

'Not Jomo?'

'No. Jomo leads the K.A.U.[2] But they both fight for the
freedom of black people.'

'I hear they kill white settlers.'

'Yes. And they kill black people who are traitors to their
country. They fight in the forest for the black people.'

'Ah, that is a fine thing to do!'

———

Ngotho lived in fear for his family, which was a family no longer.
And Ngotho knew that one day Jacobo would punish him. He
no longer hoped that he would get his land back. The land of
his fathers was lost for ever. What had he to hope for in his old
age? Would his youngest son Njoroge save them? That was his
only hope. But did Njoroge understand what was happening? Did
anyone understand?

That night, Kori came and brought them more bad news.
Jomo had been tried by the white men and he had lost his case.
Jomo, who had gone across the sea, been educated, but who stood
for custom and tradition, had failed.

The men were silent and Njeri, a woman, spoke for them all.

'The white man made the laws. He made the laws that took the
land away from us. He did not ask for our agreement, as in the old
days of the tribe. Now our leader, Jomo, tries to fight for us. But
he is taken by the white man and tried under his laws. Of course
he cannot win . . .'

And Njeri began to cry. Njoroge had never heard her speak for
such a long time.

Then Boro said, 'White people stand together and this makes
them strong. But we black people are divided against each

50

other. Now Jomo is in prison, we will become the white men's slaves. They made us fight in their wars. They took away our traditions . . .'

Boro stood up and his voice became a shout.

'We must never give in. Never! Never! Black people must rise up and fight!'

Njoroge's eyes opened wide. Njeri turned her eyes towards the door in fear. Kenya was now a land where everyone was afraid.

9

'There's no Safe Place'

M r Howlands, the District Officer, sat alone in his office. It was a small, square building with a red roof. It was surrounded by the buildings and huts of the police garrison[5]. All around was a fence of barbed wire.

He had only agreed to become District Officer to protect his land from Mau Mau. They wanted to drive him away, back to England. But who were they? Savages. Just black savages.

Before the strike, Mr Howlands had not really thought about the black workers on his land. He had not thought about their needs or their wants. But now he was willing to fight like a lion for what belonged to him.

Mr Howlands was waiting for Jacobo. Jacobo was the Chief, but a savage like the rest of them! Mr Howlands was using Jacobo to make trouble between the blacks. That would stop them fighting the white man!

There was a knock on the door and Jacobo came in. He took off his hat and smiled in the way Mr Howlands hated.

'Sit down, Jacobo. Why did you want to see me? I haven't got long. What's the matter?'

'Well, sir. It's this man, Ngotho, sir. He's a bad man. A terrible man. He has taken many oaths. And he led the strike.'

'I know all this,' Mr Howlands said. 'What has he done now?'

'This man, Ngotho, has sons. They have come back to the village. They are planning trouble – big trouble – especially the son, Boro. We should send them all to a detention camp[2]. Then we could watch Ngotho more closely. I feel sure he is the real leader of Mau Mau.'

'All right,' Mr Howlands answered. 'Arrest the sons for breaking curfew[2] or anything. Then put them in a camp.'

'Thank you, sir, thank you. I think this Mau Mau will be beaten.'

Mr Howlands did not answer. When Jacobo had gone, Mr Howlands stood by the window thinking. He had never forgotten what Ngotho had done.

A few nights later, Ngotho and his family were sitting in Nyokabi's hut. Kamau never slept at home now. Boro might be coming later. But he and Kori had their beds in Njeri's hut, a few yards away.

They sat in darkness. When they spoke, they spoke in whispers, but no one had much to say. They knew that the dark night would be long.

It was too late for Boro to come now. The curfew had begun. Njeri and Kori stood up quietly. They went out without saying goodbye. No one said goodbye nowadays in case it was for the last time. They were afraid that they might never meet again.

'Halt!' The terrible shout rang through the night. Njoroge trembled with fear. Ngotho stood up, went to the door and then walked back to his place. After a while, Nyokabi came in, crying bitterly.

'They have taken them away!' she cried.

Ngotho rushed to the door, but it was too late. What a coward! He had watched his wife and son being taken away and done nothing! He came back from the door, blaming himself for being a coward.

'Jacobo has done this,' Ngotho said at last. He wants to ruin me – to destroy this family. And he will do it.'

At that moment, Boro came in. He could see that something was wrong.

'They have taken your mother and brother away,' Ngotho told him, holding his head in shame. 'They were out after the curfew.'

'Halt!' The terrible shout rang through the night.

'Curfew . . . curfew . . .' Boro repeated. And turning towards Ngotho he said, 'And you did nothing?'

'Listen, my son . . .' Ngotho began.

Boro turned and went out. They would not see his face again for a long time.

Njeri was tried and fined for breaking the curfew. But Kori was sent to a detention camp without trial. Jacobo had not caught Ngotho, but he was willing to wait.

Now Ngotho's home was a home no longer. No stories were told there. No young people from the village met there. Only Njoroge still had faith in his father. And the more terrible conditions became, the more Njoroge believed in his education. Only education could save them now. One day he would use his learning to fight the white man. He would continue the work his father had started. Njoroge even dreamt that one day he would save his country – God's country – Kenya.

But many things still puzzled him.

'This morning,' Njoroge told his mother, 'a letter was fixed to the wall of our school. It told the headmaster to close the school. If he didn't, forty boys would have their heads cut off. Kimathi signed it.'

'Then you must stay at home,' his mother said. 'Your life is more important than education.'

'I thought Mau Mau was on the side of the black people,' Njoroge said.

'Hush,' Nyokabi whispered. 'Don't say that name!'

But Kamau told Njoroge to go back to school.

'Do you think you are safer at home?' Kamau asked. 'No. There's no safe place and no hiding-place in this land.'

So Njoroge did not leave school. But, like everyone else, he lived in fear. He was almost a young man now and things were becoming clearer in his mind. He was beginning to understand what had happened to his country.

Kamau was now the only brother still at home. He paid the

cost of Njoroge's circumcision when the time came. He bought food and clothes and paid Njoroge's school fees.

So Njoroge still felt he had a family – he had a father, a brother and two mothers. In another year, he would take the examination to enter secondary school. So he read and worked harder than ever.

10

Mwihaki

Njoroge had not seen Mwihaki since she went to the boarding school. He did not want to see her. How could he be her friend when his father and her father were enemies?

But there were times when he longed to see[5] and speak to her. He remembered her soft hands and clear eyes.

One Saturday, Njoroge went to the African shops to see his brother, Kamau.

'Is it well with you, brother?'

'It is well. How is home?'

'Everything is well at home,' replied Njoroge. 'But you look worried, brother. What's the matter?'

'Haven't you heard, Njoroge? Six men of the village were taken from their houses three nights ago. They have been found dead in the forest. You know all of them. One of them was Nganga.'

'Nganga! On whose land we have built our huts?'

'Yes.'

Njoroge could not believe he would never see the men again. Who had killed them? The white men or Mau Mau? Njoroge thought of Boro who was fighting in the forest. The thought frightened him.

A few days later, on his way home from the market, Njoroge heard someone call his name. Mwihaki was coming towards him. She was tall and graceful. Her soft, dark eyes were full of life.

She saw a tall, strong young man with a handsome face– attractive and mysterious.

'You have changed much,' Njoroge said.

'Have I? So have you. Much has happened since we last met.'

They tried to talk, but they could find little to say.

'I hope you enjoy your holidays,' Njoroge said, starting to move away. 'I must go now.'

At first Mwihaki did not answer and then she said, 'I'm so lonely here. No one wants to talk to me.'

Njoroge's heart began to beat hard. And then, suddenly, he said, 'Let's meet on Sunday in church. Let's go there together. As we used to do.'

'All right. I shall be waiting for you. Go in peace.'

When Mwihaki was walking away, Njoroge nearly called her back. He felt that they should not meet. How could he be friends with Jacobo's daughter? But on Sunday, he put on his best clothes, clean and well pressed. He was afraid, but he remembered Mwihaki's words, 'I'm so lonely here.'

Mwihaki looked very pretty in her white blouse and brown skirt. Her black hair was shining and beautiful.

She felt that the trouble between Ngotho and her father had nothing to do with her feelings for Njoroge. She had heard about Mau Mau. But she did not think anyone in the village was a member of Mau Mau.

The preacher spoke and he gave no comfort to the people. This was a time of fighting and sorrow, as the Bible told them. He could not tell them what to do.

The two young people went home along the path they used to walk together. When they were near Mwihaki's home, she said, 'Let's go in.'

Njoroge started to refuse and Mwihaki looked sad.

'I know why you don't want to come inside, but please . . .'

They went in together. Njoroge hoped that he would not meet Jacobo, but then he saw the Chief in front of him.

Njoroge sat quietly, looking at the family photographs on the walls. Jacobo and his homeguards[2] sat down too. Jacobo looked tired and his face was older. He asked Njoroge about his education and said, 'I hope you do well. It is boys like you who must work hard and rebuild the country.'

Njoroge, in a moment of joy, saw himself rebuilding the whole country. Then he saw the homeguards staring at him. He remembered the village men who had died.

Later, Njoroge and Mwihaki sat together on the hill near their homes.

'When the preacher spoke about the end of the world, I was afraid,' Mwihaki said quietly. 'It is very hard to think of all this country being destroyed.'

'That's what the Bible says,' Njoroge said.

'And all this trouble in our country. Do you think Jesus knew it would happen? If he did, he could have stopped it.'

'Everything will be all right in the end,' Njoroge said softly. 'God will help us.'

'The thing that worries me most is how my father has changed,' Mwihaki said. 'He never talks to me now. And the guns he carries make me afraid of him. People don't talk to me, you know, even girls of my age. It is, oh . . .' and to Njoroge's horror, Mwihaki burst into tears.

Njoroge looked away down towards the plain below them. Would he really be able to help his country?

'You know, I think the people have sinned. If one man sins, God punishes all.' Then, looking at Mwihaki, Njoroge went on firmly, 'Peace shall come to this land.'

'Oh, Njoroge, do you really think so?'

'Yes. Sunshine always follows a dark night[1].'

Mwihaki opened her eyes wide.

'Shall we go away from here and come back when the dark night is over?'

'But . . .'

'It is a good idea, isn't it?'

'No, no,' said Njoroge. 'How could we leave our parents? And where would we go and what could we eat?'

Mwihaki laughed, 'I was only joking.'

Njoroge felt he would never understand this girl.

'Of course. I knew you were joking,' said Njoroge.

'When I come back from school, you will be my friend, won't you?'

Njoroge smiled at the girl who was like a sister to him.

'When you come back, I shall be with you. That is a promise. And remember, the sun will rise tomorrow[1].'

They walked back down the hill together before the dark night came. The boy and the girl went forward, thinking their own thoughts. For a time, they forgot about the darkness over their land.

11

'Will There Ever be Freedom?'

Mr Howlands was very pleased. His plans were working. Blacks were destroying blacks. Let them! What did he care? Mr Howlands was enjoying his work and for a while he had forgotten about farming.

Mr Howlands looked up from his desk at Chief Jacobo. More than ever, he wanted to kick him. But the time for that had not yet come.

'Are you sure it's Boro who is the leader of the gang?' Mr Howlands asked.

'I'm not sure, but the man is dangerous, as you know. I think he sometimes comes home. Even if he doesn't, Ngotho must know where he is hiding.'

'Then go on watching Ngotho and tell me what he does.'

Mr Howlands knew that one day Ngotho would be arrested. When that happened, his work would be over. He would go back to the farm.

Jacobo took a piece of paper from his pocket. He held it out for Mr Howlands to read.

Stop – or we will have your head.

This is our last warning.

'You fool,' he said to Jacobo. 'Have you received messages before and not told me?'

'Yes – two. But . . .'

'Are they from Ngotho?'

'They must be. A few months ago, his youngest son was at my house – with my daughter . . .'

Mr Howlands did not understand.

'All right,' he said quickly. 'Leave this paper with me. Never go out without a guard. Watch Ngotho. New huts are being built

61

Jacobo took a piece of paper from his pocket.

here in the garrison. When they are finished, you can move into the compound with your family.'

———

Boro now lived in the forest as a leader of the Freedom Fighters. Boro was daring and brave because he did not care what happened to him. He believed in nothing except revenge[5]. He no longer thought about the land his family had lost. Too many of his loved ones had died.

When Boro's lieutenant[2] spoke of Freedom, Boro answered bitterly, 'Freedom? Will there ever be Freedom for you and me?'

'Why do we fight then, if not for Freedom?'

'To kill. It's kill or be killed. We kill, the white man kills. Fighting is the only way.'

'But surely we are fighting for a cause[2]. And our cause is Freedom.'

'Maybe. But Freedom can't bring back my brother. So I kill and rejoice when I kill. Chief Jacobo will be next. He must die. He has ignored the warnings we sent him.'

'And Mr Howlands? What about him?'

'Yes, he is a dangerous man. He will die too, but not yet. Jacobo must be shot first.'

'Who's going to do it?'

'I will,' Boro said quietly. 'I must. This is revenge for my family.'

———

Throughout the troubled time, the people still believed in education. Boro, Ngotho and even Jacobo – they all believed in education.

When Njoroge passed his examinations for High School, the news went quickly from hill to hill. Many people gave him money to help him to continue his studies. He was not only Ngotho's son, but the son of the land.

Before he went to Siriana Secondary School, Njoroge saw Mwihaki again. They had not met for a year, but Mwihaki had changed very little.

'When people go away, they sometimes forget their friends,' Mwihaki said to Njoroge.

'Do they?'

'Yes. But what are you going to do with your life, Njoroge? One day you will be an important man.'

'I don't know. Maybe I'll go to Britain or America. It doesn't matter.'

Njoroge glanced at Mwihaki who was looking down at the ground sadly. Was she jealous of his success?

'Our country needs us all,' Njoroge said. 'It needs me. It needs you. When this trouble is over, we must all get together to rebuild the country. Your father told me that and I have never forgotten it.'

'But the country is so dark now,' Mwihaki whispered. 'There is fear in the air. Not fear of death, but fear of living.'

'The sun will rise tomorrow,' Njoroge replied.

'Tomorrow, tomorrow! What is "tomorrow" – what is "the country" – what does it all mean to you?'

Njoroge saw the anger in Mwihaki's eyes and he was a little afraid.

'Don't be angry, Mwihaki,' he said. 'We must have hope. Bloodshed and death will not go on for ever. Think of the future – of that sweet, sunny day when, with God's help, we can all live freely again.'

Mwihaki was quiet now.

'Come,' Njoroge said. 'The sun is going down. We must go home.'

64

When they parted, Njoroge said, 'Thank you, Mwihaki. You have been like a sister to me.'

She watched him go. Then she wiped away her tears and turned towards her home. She ran back – faster and faster . . .

12

The House of Pain

Siriana Secondary School was one of the best schools in the country. For the first time, Njoroge was taught by white men. They were friendly and helpful and at first this confused him.

The school was a place of peace. Boys from many tribes became friends and worked together. Njoroge worked hard. His trust in God grew stronger every day. The school often played games with boys from other schools. One day, the Hill School, which was for European boys, sent a football team to play a match.

One of the boys was tall, with long, brown hair. Njoroge was sure he had seen him before, near home. The boy looked at Njoroge and said, 'I remember you. You are the son of Ngotho who . . .' The boy stopped and then added, 'My name is Stephen – Stephen Howlands.'

'I am Njoroge.'

They walked together in silence. Then Njoroge said, 'I used to see you when we were little boys. I was afraid of you then.'

Stephen smiled.

'Yes, I was afraid of you too. People fear each other because they have been taught to fear each other. That's bad, but we can't get away from it.'

'The land is dark now,' Njoroge said. 'But the future will be different.'

'I'm going away soon,' Stephen went on. 'I'm going to England.'

'Of course, England's your home.'

'No it isn't,' Stephen answered quickly. 'I was born here. I have never been to England and I don't want to go there now.'

Njoroge felt sorry for the white boy. At least he, Njoroge, could stay in Kenya. That was his home.

'Father is staying here,' Stephen added. 'But somehow I feel I'll never come back. I'll never see my father again.'

The boys stood in silence. Njoroge did not want to think about Mr Howlands.

'Let's watch the game,' Njoroge said at last. But when they reached the football field, the two boys walked off in different directions. Once more, they seemed afraid to talk to each other.

––––––

One cold morning, in Njoroge's third term at Siriana, he got up as usual and said his prayers. His first class was English. He felt very happy and laughed and talked with his friends.

'My mother tells me that a man should not be too happy in the morning,' one boy said. 'It's a bad omen. Something bad is sure to happen.'

Njoroge did not want to believe this. But he had been having bad dreams all week. He decided he would write to Mwihaki that night.

Then the lesson began and Njoroge forgot his troubles. He was answering a question when the headmaster came in and called him out of the class.

Njoroge's heart began to beat fast. He saw a black police car. Two police officers were standing in the headmaster's room. The headmaster made them wait outside his room and told Njoroge to sit down.

'I'm sorry to hear this news about your family,' the headmaster said. 'It's a bad business and you are wanted at home. Remember that whatever your family has made you do, God will look after you. I know you will not forget our teaching.'

Njoroge went to the police car, confused and unhappy. The police did not take him home, but to the homeguard post[2] known as the House of Pain.

Njoroge went to the police car, confused and unhappy.

The following day, he was questioned by two European officers.

'What's your name? . . . How old are you?'

'Have you taken the Oath?'

'No!'

'Say "sir",' shouted one of the guards.

'No, sir.'

'How many oaths have you taken?'

'None, sir.'

'How many oaths have you taken?'

One of the men moved swiftly. He hit Njoroge hard and for a moment everything went dark.

'Have you taken the Oath?'

'No oaths, sir, none. I am a schoolboy.'

Another blow and another. Tears rolled down Njoroge's face. He remembered the peace and calm of the school. It was lost for ever.

'Do you know Boro?'

'He's my brother . . .'

'Where is he?'

'I . . . don't . . . know . . .'

The officer hit him again. Then Njoroge was on the floor.

'Bloody Mau Mau!' one of the men shouted.

'Take him out!'

Njoroge was carried out by the two homeguards at the door. He was senseless. He was covered with blood where heavy boots had kicked him.

He woke up in the middle of the night. A woman was screaming in another hut. Could it be Njeri or Nyokabi?

Njoroge was taken back to the room the next day. His body was bruised and covered with blood.

'Have you taken the Oath?' the men asked.

Njoroge did not know what to say. If he told a lie, would they stop hitting him?

This time, Mr Howlands was there and he asked questions too.

'Tell the truth. If you tell the truth, we will let you go.'

But still Njoroge whispered, 'No . . .'

'Who murdered Jacobo?'

Njoroge began to shake.

'Jacobo murdered? By whom?'

'You tell us that,' Mr Howlands said.

'Me, sir? But . . .'

'Yes, you tell us.'

Mr Howlands moved nearer to Njoroge. He had a pair of pincers[5] in his hand.

'I'll show you,' he said. 'You'll be castrated[5], like your father.'

Mr Howlands began to press with the pincers and Njoroge screamed with pain.

'Tell us. Who told you to go to Jacobo's house to get information?'

But Njoroge could not hear. The pain was so bad. Mr Howlands went on asking his questions and every time he pressed harder with the pincers.

'Your father says he murdered Jacobo.'

Njoroge screamed and screamed. Then suddenly he fell to the ground.

Mr Howlands looked down at the boy he had tortured. As he walked out, the two white officers looked at each other and laughed aloud. Njoroge was not hurt again. In a few days, he was well. Then he and his two mothers were allowed to go home.

Now Njoroge's mind was full of fear[4]. His family was breaking up and he could not stop it. He thought of Mwihaki and he felt guilty. He was to blame. He felt that he had caused all this trouble by being her friend. Njoroge hated the dead chief Jacobo even more. He cried with fear, but he did not pray.

13

Two Deaths

Ngotho was kept in the homeguard post in a small hut without light. He did not know if it was day or night. To him, night and day were the same. He was in terrible pain. He was not able to sleep. He felt that he had failed his children and failed himself.

But, in spite of the pain, Ngotho was not sorry that Jacobo was dead. Two days after Jacobo had been killed, Kamau had been arrested for the murder. For a day and a half, Ngotho hesitated. He was not able to make up his mind. Then he walked into Mr Howlands' office and told him that he had killed Jacobo. The whole village had been shocked.

Ngotho was tortured for many days, but he did not change his story.

Mr Howlands was now nearly mad with hatred. Even the homeguards were afraid to watch him questioning Ngotho. But Mr Howlands got nothing more from him. All Ngotho would say was that he had killed Jacobo.

Njoroge never forgot the day his father came home. Ngotho was unable to walk and his face was covered with cuts and bruises. For four days, his eyes and mouth never opened.

His wives, Nyokabi and Njeri, wept to see their broken husband. At last, he opened his eyes and looked around the hut. Tears covered his face. When he saw Njoroge, he struggled to speak.

'You are here . . .'

'Yes, Father.'

'Why are you not at school? Have you come to laugh at your own father?'

'No, Father, no. You have given us everything. What could we do without you?'

Ngotho went on talking, but his thoughts were confused.

'Did I shoot him? I don't know. But I wanted him dead. The white men want my sons, they want young blood. They took Mwangi in the Big War. Now they've taken Kamau. And where are my other sons? Only you are here. Get back to school! Learn everything, then they can't hurt you.'

'Who's that at the door? Ah! It's Mr Howlands . . . he wants my heart . . . Boro – Boro went away. He knew! I've been a useless father.'

Then suddenly, Boro was in the hut. His hair was long and untidy. He knelt by his father's bed.

'Forgive me, Father,' Boro said. 'I didn't know.'

'So you've come back to laugh at me too. But I only meant good for you all. Stay with me now . . .'

'But I have to fight,' Boro said. 'I must go on fighting. I can't stay here. I can't!'

For a moment, Ngotho spoke more clearly.

'You must stay,' he said firmly.

'No, Father. But forgive me before I go.'

With a great effort, Ngotho sat up and put his hand on Boro's head.

'All right. Fight well. Peace to you all. And you, Njoroge, look after your mo . . .'

Ngotho fell back onto the bed.

Boro stood up.

'I should have come before,' he whispered. Then, with one last look round the hut, he ran out into the night.

They turned back to Ngotho. But he too had gone, never to return.

———

That same night, Mr Howlands was sitting in his office, waiting to go out on night patrol[2]. He enjoyed these patrols. They gave him a feeling of power and strength

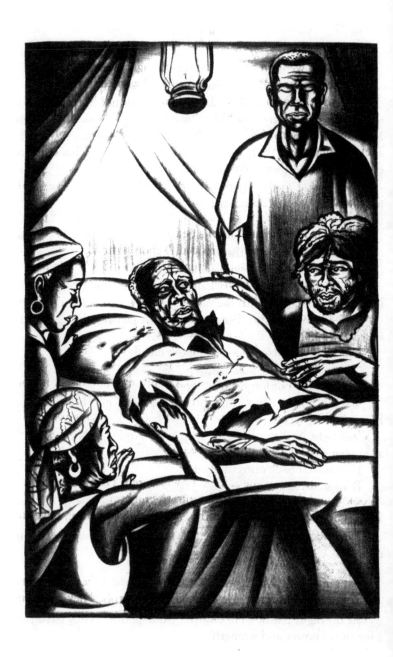

'Forgive me, Father,' Boro said. 'I didn't know.'

Mr Howlands looked at his watch. The policemen who were to go with him would soon arrive. Mr Howlands had forgotten to lock the office door. It opened and he looked round. A gun was pointing at his head.

'You move and you are dead. Now put up your hands. I killed Jacobo,' Boro said.

'I know.'

'Jacobo betrayed black people and helped you to kill them. You raped our women. You killed my father. You took our land.'

'This is *my* land,' Mr Howlands replied.

'Your land? Then, you white dog, you'll *die* on your land.'

Boro fired once and Mr Howlands fell to the ground. Boro rushed out into the compound, firing at the police who were all round him. Escape was impossible, but Boro was full of joy.

'He's dead,' he told them. 'The white men taught me to shoot well.'

14

His Last Hope . . .

Njoroge had to leave school. Money was badly needed at home and he had to work. He found a job in one of the Indian shops in Kippanga. But he could not do the work properly. His life was one long bad dream. His brothers, Boro and Kamau, were both in prison, accused of murdering Mr Howlands.

When little children came into the shop with their happy, hopeful faces, Njoroge thought of his own happy childhood. He thought of his education which would never be completed.

Njoroge now moved and spoke like an old man. His staring, unhappy eyes frightened the children. After less than a month, he was dismissed from his job. As he walked home to Njeri and Nyokabi, he thought only of Mwihaki. He knew he had to see and speak to her.

Mwihaki had heard about her father's death while she was at school. She had come home at once, crying as never before[3].

Njoroge sent her a note, but she decided that she could not meet him. She felt she would be betraying her dead father.

But then she remembered Njoroge's words: 'The sun will rise tomorrow.' She agreed to see Njoroge.

It was late in the afternoon when they met. When Njoroge saw Mwihaki, he knew what she meant to him. She meant more to him than anything else in the world.

'I have come,' were Mwihaki's first words. 'Tell me what you want to say.' And she turned away her face so that Njoroge did not see her tears.

'Mwihaki,' he said. 'I have lost everything – my education, my faith and my family. You have always meant so much to me. I feel guilty. I feel I am to blame for what my people have done to you. I wanted to meet you and say that I am sorry.'

She meant more to him than anything else in the world.

'You didn't warn me that my father was in danger.'

'I knew nothing. And now I know there will be no tomorrow[3]. You are my only hope – I love you. But you have good reason to feel only hate for me.'

He took her hand and now her tears flowed freely.

'Don't, don't . . .' said Mwihaki.

'Mwihaki, I love you. Save me. Without you I am lost. Let us go away from here – together!'

'No, no. You must save me. We cannot go away now. We must stay to build our country.'

'But we must go. Kenya is no place for us.'

'We are no longer children. We must wait. The sun will rise tomorrow,' Mwihaki told him.

'All that was a dream,' he said. 'We can only live today.'

'But we both have our duty,' Mwihaki said. 'I cannot leave my mother. Let's wait for a new day.'

Mwihaki had won. She walked away. Njoroge's last hope had gone. He fell to the ground crying, 'Mwihaki, Mwihaki!'

———

On the following Sunday, Njoroge walked out alone into the fields. Nyokabi watched him leave the hut. She wanted to stop him. She wanted to speak to him. But neither she nor Njeri knew what to say to him.

Njoroge walked in a dream – a dream of fear and sadness. He thought of his dead father. He thought of Boro, waiting to die. Kamau was in prison for life and Kori was somewhere in a detention camp.

Oh, God! But there was no God now, there was nothing. Even his love, his last hope had left him.

Njoroge walked on, listening to the voice inside his head. *Go on. Go on.*

And then, *Wait for the night . . .*

He had reached the place where he had said goodbye to

Mwihaki. He took the rope out of his pocket and laughed quietly. He waited for the darkness.

. . . And now night covered him.

The rope was ready, hanging from the tree. As he took it in his hands, he heard a cry, 'Njoroge!'

Njoroge only laughed and prepared himself for what he had to do.

'Njoroge!'

The voice was clear. Njoroge's heart beat faster. His mother was looking for him. He stood there for a moment and then his courage left him. He heard the loved voice again and now he could see a light. His mother came towards him, carrying a burning piece of wood to light the way.

'Mother, I am here.'

'Njoroge.' She held him close. 'Let's go home,' she said.

Njoroge followed her. He remembered the last words of his father – his father had asked him to look after the women.

He remembered Mwihaki's words. She had asked him to wait for a new day, but he had not.

They met Njeri who had also come to find him, in spite of the curfew laws. Njoroge heard the voice in his head again.

You are a coward. You have always been a coward. Why didn't you do it?

And Njoroge repeated aloud, 'Why didn't I do it?'

The voice answered: *Because you are a coward.*

Yes, he whispered to himself. I am a coward.

And he ran home and opened the door for his two mothers.

Points for Understanding

1

1 'Would you like to go to school?' she said.
   (a)   Who said these words?
   (b)   What was Njoroge's reaction?
2 Why would Njoroge not be able to get food at midday?
3 What words tell you that the young boy thought education was very important?
4 'Don't worry about me,' Kamau said to the little boy.
   (a)   Who was Kamau?
   (b)   Why should Njoroge not worry about Kamau?
5 What did Njoroge think would happen if he got educated?
6 Who was Ngotho? How many wives did he have? What were their names?
7 What was the name of Njoroge's older brother? How had he died?
8 This land I hand over to you, O Man and Woman.
   (a)   Who did God give the land to in the beginning?
   (b)   Who had taken the land from them?
9 What had the British given the Kenyans in return for their help in the First Big War?
10 A bitter anger filled Boro's heart.
   (a)   Who was Boro?
   (b)   What had Boro done in the Second Big War?
   (c)   Why was Boro angry with Ngotho?
   (d)   What words of Boro's tell you that his patience was coming to an end?

2

1 Mwihaki showed Njoroge the way to school.
   (a)   Who was Mwihaki's father?
   (b)   Which land did he own?
   (c)   Why was Mwihaki's father a rich man?
2 Why was Nyokabi angry when she found Njoroge playing with Mwihaki?
3 Why did Nyokabi want Njoroge to get a white man's education?
4 Why was Njoroge ashamed of meeting Mwihaki?
5 Why was Nganga a rich man?

81

6 Why did Kamau hate Nganga?
7 Explain what Kamau meant by the words: 'Sometimes a European is better than an African.'

3

1 Ngotho was thinking of what his son Boro had said.
    (a)   What had Boro said?
    (b)   What questions was Ngotho beginning to ask himself?
2 Nothing mattered to Mr Howlands except the shamba.
    (a)   What was the shamba?
    (b)   What kind of person was Mr Howlands' wife?
    (c)   Why was she not able to get rid of Ngotho?
3 Describe Mr Howlands.
4 Mr Howlands said something which had two meanings.
    (a)   What did Mr Howlands say?
    (b)   What did Ngotho think Mr Howlands meant?
    (c)   What had Mr Howlands really meant?
    (d)   What could Ngotho not understand?
5 Why did Ngotho think that Mr Howlands had no right to complain?

4

1 Who said: 'Education is the light of Kenya'? What do you think this means?
2 Ngotho told Njoroge that education was everything. But what did he really believe?
3 Why did Ngotho work so hard for Mr Howlands?
4 Why had Boro and Kori left home? Where had they gone?
5 Why was Boro angry with Ngotho? Why did he hate the white man?
6 What was Kamau not sure about?
7 Why were the black people going on strike?
8 Why was Jomo Kenyatta known as the Black Moses?
9 Where did Njoroge hope to go to complete his education?

5

1 A white woman came to the school.
   (a) Why did the teacher beat the children after the white woman had gone?
   (b) Who was the white woman's father?
   (c) Why did Njoroge think that perhaps she was different from her father?
2 What did Njoroge think would happen if Kamau went to Nairobi?
3 Why did Njoroge's visit to his brother make him work harder at school?
4 What did Njoroge believe the future of his family and of his village depended on?
5 Why was Njoroge not able to explain his beliefs to Mwihaki?

6

1 What was different about the young men that Kori and Boro brought home with them from the city?
2 Who did Njoroge think the black people were? Who was going to lead them to the Promised Land?
3 Who were going on strike?
4 What were the strikers going to ask for?
5 What did Njoroge dream about after he fell asleep?
6 What did Mr Howlands threaten to do if any of his workers went on strike?
7 Why could Ngotho not decide whether to strike or not?
8 Why were Ngotho and Nyokabi quarrelling?
9 Njoroge waited in the dark for God's answer.
   (a) What question did Njoroge ask God?
   (b) What was the answer?

7

1 Each wanted to tell their parents the good news.
   (a) What was the good news?
   (b) How did Mwihaki's mother react to the news?
   (c) Why did Njoroge forget his good news?
2 Describe the strike meeting. What part did Jacobo play at the meeting? What part did Ngotho play?

3 How had Ngotho harmed himself?
4 Did the strike succeed or fail?
5 Who helped Ngotho?
6 What happened to Mwihaki?
7 How was Njoroge able to continue his education?

8

1 Who was Dedan Kimathi and what stories were told about him? Do you think the stories were true?
2 Many things had changed. Give examples of the changes in the lives of Jacobo and Ngotho.
3 What did education mean to many children in Kenya?
4 What had happened to Kori? How had he escaped?
5 What did Kori think would happen if Jomo won his case?
6 Why did Boro no longer respect his father?
7 What did Ngotho refuse to do? What was the reason for his refusal?
8 What reasons does Njeri give for Jomo's failure in court?
9 Why did Njeri turn her eyes towards the door in fear?

9

1 Why had Mr Howlands agreed to become District Officer?
2 What did Mr Howlands really think of Jacobo?
3 What orders did Mr Howlands give to Jacobo?
4 Why did Jacobo tell Mr Howlands that Ngotho was the real leader of Mau Mau?
5 Describe the arrest of Njeri and Kori.
6 Why did Ngotho blame himself?
7 What happened to Kori?
8 Why did Njoroge live in fear?
9 How did Kamau help Njoroge?

10

1 Why could Njoroge not remain friends with Mwihaki? Why did he long to see her?
2 Whose dead body was found in the forest? How many others had been killed? Who had killed them?

3 Why did Njoroge agree to meet Mwihaki?
4 Why did Njoroge agree to go into Jacobo's house?
5 How had Jacobo changed?
6 What did Mwihaki suggest she and Njoroge should do? Why did Njoroge not agree?

11

1 Why were Mr Howlands' plans working well?
2 Jacobo told Mr Howlands that he had received a threatening message.
   (a) What was written on the piece of paper?
   (b) How many messages had Jacobo received?
   (c) Why did Jacobo say that the messages were from Ngotho?
3 Did Boro believe he was fighting for Freedom? What was the only thing he was interested in?
4 Describe the meeting between Mwihaki and Njoroge. Who had no hope for the future? Who still had hope?

12

1 Njoroge met Stephen Howlands at a football match with another school.
   (a) Why did Stephen think people were afraid of each other?
   (b) Why did Stephen not want to go to England?
   (c) Why did Njoroge feel sorry for Stephen?
2 Which homeguard post was Njoroge taken to?
3 Why did the police question Njoroge about taking oaths?
4 What did the police want to know about Boro?
5 How did Mr Howlands treat Njoroge?
6 What had happened to Jacobo?
7 Why did the police think Njoroge had gone to Jacobo's house?
8 Who else had been in the homeguard post?
9 Why did Njoroge feel guilty?

13

1 Why did Ngotho confess to the murder of Jacobo?
2 Why were the homeguards afraid to watch Mr Howlands questioning Ngotho?

3 Why do you think Mr Howlands released Ngotho?
4 Boro came to see Ngotho before he died.
  (a) What did Boro ask from his father?
  (b) What did Ngotho ask Boro to do?
  (c) What was Boro's reply?
5 Describe how Boro killed Mr Howlands.

14

1 Why did Njoroge have to leave school?
2 Why was Njoroge dismissed from his job in the Indian shop?
3 Compare the meeting between Njoroge and Mwihaki in this
  chapter with the meeting in Chapter Eleven. What is the main
  difference?
4 The rope was ready, hanging from the tree.
  (a) What was Njoroge planning to do?
  (b) Who stopped him?
5 Njoroge remembered the words of Ngotho and Mwihaki.
  (a) What had been Ngotho's last words to Njoroge?
  (b) What had Mwihaki said to Njoroge?
6 What do you think Njoroge will do in the future?

Glossary

SECTION 1
Terms to do with light and darkness

The author uses ideas of light and darkness throughout the story. Light is used to suggest hope, freedom and a happy future. Darkness is used to suggest despair, imprisonment and a miserable future.

home – *bring light to our home* (page 26)
> Ngotho believes that an educated person will bring wealth and happiness to the family.

Kenya – *Education is the light of Kenya* (page 26)
> this comes from a speech by Jomo Kenyatta. Jomo Kenyatta believed that Kenya's future success depended on education.

mind – *was like a bright light in Njoroge's mind* (page 13)
> Njoroge thought that education would bring success and happiness in the future. This hope of Njoroge's is described as 'a bright light' in his mind.

night – *sunshine always follows a dark night* (page 59)
> night is seen as a time of despair and sorrow. But when the sun rises and brings a new day, it also brings with it hope for a better future.

tomorrow – *the sun will rise tomorrow* (page 60)
> see *night* above.

SECTION 2
Terms to do with political systems and government

The background to the political system in Kenya is explained in the note on the historical background on page 5.

Army – *African Freedom Army* (page 47)
> see the note on the historical background on page 5.

camp – *detention camp* (page 52)
> Kenyans who fought against British rule were arrested by the police and kept prisoner in a detention camp.

case – *win his case* (page 48)

Kenyans believed that Jomo Kenyatta would win the fight for Kenya to gain independence from Britain. A case is a matter taken to a court for its decision. To win a case is to prove that you are right.

cause – *fighting for a cause* (page 63)

to fight for a cause is to fight for something you believe to be right and just.

crop – *cash crop* (page 17)

a crop grown by a farmer which can easily be sold for a good price in the market. The main cash crops of Kenya are coffee and tea.

curfew – *breaking curfew* (page 52)

a curfew is a law which says that every person must be indoors by a certain time. Any one found on the street after that time can be arrested and taken to prison.

custom – *against the custom* (page 42)

a custom is the way something is done over a long period of time. Against the custom means doing something in a very different way.

Empire – *British Empire* (page 38)

until the Second World War, Britain ruled a great number of countries. All these countries were part of the British Empire. Kenya was in the British Empire until the Second World War. It was a British colony until it became independent in 1963. It was ruled by white men from England. Africans did not govern their own country at this time.

Forest – *Freedom Boys of the Forest* (page 47)

an organization also called 'Mau Mau' or 'Kenya Land and Freedom Army'. See the note on the historical background on page 5.

homeguard (page 58)

the homeguard were Kenyans employed by the British as policemen. They were used by the British to arrest other Kenyans. The homeguard were hated by the Kenyans and were looked on as traitors because they were fighting against their own people. See *traitors* below.

K.A.U. (page 50)

Kenyan African Union – see the note on the historical background on page 5.

Kenyatta – *Jomo Kenyatta* (page 26)

see the note on the historical background on page 5.

lieutenant (page 63)
   a junior officer in an army.
Mau Mau (page 48)
   see the note on the historical background on page 5.
Oath – *taking oath* (page 48)
   see the note on the historical background on page 5.
Officer – *District Officer* (page 47)
   a British official who had full powers to rule over the part of the
   country he lived in.
patrol – *night patrol* (page 73)
   policemen who go out together at night looking for Mau Mau or for
   anyone caught breaking the curfew. See *curfew* above.
post – *homeguard post* (page 67)
   a building which the homeguard used as a headquarters and as a
   prison. Prisoners were often tortured in the homeguard posts. See
   homeguard above.
settler – *white settler* (page 21)
   the climate in Kenya, especially in the White Highlands is very
   pleasant. After the Second World War, many British people came
   to live in Kenya and the colonial government gave them land
   where they could build houses and make farms. The best land was
   taken from the Kenyans who owned it and given to the white
   settlers.
taxes (page 38)
   money paid by the people to the government. The government uses
   the money to run the country.
traitor (page 39)
   a traitor is someone who works against his or her own people. See
   homeguard above.
unemployment (page 33)
   a time when people cannot find any work.

SECTION 3
Unusual negative forms

The negative in English is usually formed by 'not' or 'never' with the
verb – e.g. 'Jomo Kenyatta was never a member of Mau Mau.' But there
are other ways of forming the negative. These other forms are often
used to give greater emphasis.

before – *crying as never before* (page 76)

can also be expressed as 'she cried as she had never cried before'.

calico – *nothing but a piece of calico* (page 13)

can also be expressed as 'he was not wearing anything except a piece of calico'.

first – *not all of it at first* (page 14)

can also be expressed as 'At first, they did not take all the land.'

lifetime – *'Perhaps not in my lifetime'* (page 15)

can also be expressed as 'Perhaps the day will not come until after I am dead.'

tomorrow – *no tomorrow* (page 78)

can also be expressed as 'Tomorrow will not come.'

SECTION 4
Terms to do with emotions

The story is set in Kenya at a time of fierce struggle when people felt very strong emotions. The Kenyans wanted freedom from colonial rule. The British – especially the white settlers – did not want to lose control of the land they were living in. Many different emotions are written about in the story: bitter anger, despair, joy and hope. Some of these expressions are listed below.

anger – *bitter anger* (page 15)

fear – *full of fear* (page 71)

hate – *full of hate* (page 27)

hope – *filled with hope* (page 24)

joy – *filled with joy* (page 27)

SECTION 5
General

bewitch (page 35)

to bewitch someone is to use magic to put a spell on a person so that they behave in a strange way.

blame (page 27)

to blame someone is to say that they are responsible for something bad which has happened.

boy (page 21)

the name used by whites when talking to African servants.

Bwana (page 21)
> an African word meaning 'boss' or 'master'.

castrated (page 71)
> to castrate is to remove the sexual organs of a man or male animal.

circumcision (page 56)
> circumcision is an operation to remove a piece of skin from the end of a man's sexual organ. This operation is often done for religious reasons. Njoroge was circumcised to show he had grown from a boy into a man.

comfort (page 35)
> to make someone feel better or happier by holding them in your arms.

coward (page 21)
> someone who is afraid to do what they believe ought to be done.

disillusioned (page 43)
> you become disillusioned when you are not able to believe that there is any hope for a better future.

farms (page 15)
> to farm is to work the land and grow crops.

garrison (page 52)
> a building where soldiers live. Usually a garrison is a strong building which can easily be defended by the soldiers.

God – *chosen people of God* (page 32)
> in the Bible, the Jews believed that they were the chosen people of God. They believed that God had sent them Moses to lead them out of slavery to the Promised Land. Many Kenyans believed that Jomo Kenyatta was like Moses and that he would lead the Kenyans out of the slavery of colonial rule.

harsh (page 20)
> cruel.

heart (page 32)
> Njoroge had many thoughts in his mind, but he was not able to tell anyone what he was thinking.

hour – *hero of the hour* (page 39)
> a hero for a very short time . After the excitement was over, the villagers realized that what Ngotho had done was wrong and foolish.

mind – *make up his mind* (page 34) *changed his mind* (page 35)
> to make up your mind is to make a decision to do something. To change your mind is to decide to do something else.

missionary (page 24)

a missionary is someone who goes to a foreign land to tell people about his or her religion. There were many Christian missionaries in Kenya during the British colonial rule. Many white settlers believed that white people were better than black people, but the missionaries taught that all men were equal.

pincers (page 71)

a metal tool usually used for holding and pulling nails, etc.

pyrethrum (page 17)

a plant which is used to make medicine. The plant was valuable and was sold for cash. See *cash crop* in Section 2 above.

revenge (page 63)

to do harm to someone who has done harm to you.

reward (page 32)

the opposite of punish. The missionaries taught that God would punish bad people by sending them to hell and reward good people by accepting them into heaven.

rumour (page 47)

a story which people tell each other. A rumour goes quickly from one person to another and it may be true or untrue.

see – *long to see* (page 57)

to have a great wish to see someone.

shame – *bring shame on us* (page 13)

if you do something wrong and people hear about it, it brings shame on you and on your family.

strike (page 28)

a time when workers will not work because they want more money or are angry about something.

tear-gas (page 39)

a gas which burns people's eyes and makes it difficult for them to breathe. Tear-gas is often used by police to break up crowds in a riot.

tease (page 17)

to make fun of someone.

trade (page 13)

a trade is a job which requires skills with your hands, like a carpenter, a plumber, etc.

village – *elders of the village* (page 33)

the wise, older men of the village.

Of Mice and Men *by John Steinbeck*
Bleak House *by Charles Dickens*
The Great Ponds *by Elechi Amadi*
Rebecca *by Daphne du Maurier*
Our Mutual Friend *by Charles Dickens*
The Grapes of Wrath *by John Steinbeck*
The Return of the Native *by Thomas Hardy*
Weep Not, Child *by Ngugi wa Thiong'o*
Precious Bane *by Mary Webb*
Mine Boy *by Peter Abrahams*

For further information on the full selection of Readers
at all five levels in the series, please refer to the
Heinemann Readers catalogue.

Published by Macmillan Heinemann ELT
Between Towns Road, Oxford OX4 3PP
Macmillan Heinemann ELT is an imprint of
Macmillan Publishers Limited
Companies and representatives throughout the world
Heinemann is a registered trademark of Harcourt Education, used under licence.

ISBN 978–1–4050–7331–8

Weep Not, Child © Ngũgĩ wa Thiong'o 1964
First published 1964
First published by Heinemann Educational Books Ltd in the African
Writers Series 1964

This retold version by Margaret Tarner for Macmillan Readers
First published 1988
Text © Margaret Tarner 1988, 1992

This edition first published 2005

Typography by Adrian Hodgkins
Cover illustration by Dolores Fairman

Printed in Thailand

2011 2010 2009 2008 2007
11   10   9   8   7   6